HOWARD HAD A HOT AIR BALLOON

STEVE LAWHEAD

A LION PICTURE STORY

Tring · Batavia · Sydney

Howard was a boy who enjoyed adventures whenever he could get them — which was more often than you might expect.

"How would you like to see a balloon race?" his father asked, one bright and breezy morning.

That was all Howard needed to hear. At once, they were hurrying off to the park. There, just as his father had said, were twenty huge hot air balloons — some already drifting away.

"Wonderful!" shouted Howard, and he ran to the
nearest one for a closer look. Just at that moment,
however, the balloon broke free and the wind caught it.

Howard dashed for the trailing rope, but the wind
puffed, the balloon swayed, the basket swung toward
him, and Howard was scooped up just that quick.

The next thing Howard knew, he was floating up,
up, and away into the clear blue sky.

"Howard, come back!" shouted his father.

"Whoa!" laughed Howard. "I'm going for a ride!"

Since there was nothing else he could do, Howard's father called, "Well, have a good time, my boy. And try to stay out of trouble."

"I will," said Howard, as the balloon climbed higher. In no time at all Howard was so high above the ground he could see from one end of town to the other.

Down below were fields and meadows dotted with cows and sheep. All was green with growing things — green trees and grass as far as the eye could see — which was pretty far, because Howard was very high up. And going higher all the time.

The big balloon caught the wind like a sail and away it went. Soon he saw the great wide ocean stretching from horizon to horizon.

It was so quiet he could hear something splashing in the water far below. He looked and saw the huge dark shapes of killer whales, leaping and diving. It looked as if they were having such fun, Howard decided to join them.

He skimmed low over the water, watching the playful whales, and wondering how animals so big could be so graceful. God made them for swimming, he decided; and water was their perfect home.

Howard pulled on the red handle and the balloon went up. I wonder what I'll see next? he thought.

The wind carried him fast and far. And when he looked down again the land below had changed once more. Now it was dark green with huge leafy plants of all shapes and sizes. Jungle!

I've always wanted to explore a jungle, thought Howard, watching the thick tangle of trees and vines slide away beneath him.

Inside the balloon's basket, Howard discovered that his seat was really a travel chest. Among the things inside the chest, he found a jungle helmet and a pair of binoculars.

Howard put them on just as the balloon bumped down in a clearing. Scrambling out of the basket, he tied the balloon to a bush and then peered out at the strange environment.

Howard heard a faint buzzing noise. He fixed his
binoculars on a bush that was covered with pink
flowers, and at one of the flowers was the smallest bird
he had ever seen — beating its wings so fast they made
a thrumming sound in the air.

"Now I know why they are called hummingbirds,"
said Howard. "They really do hum."

The hummingbird fits the jungle perfectly.

Even the biggest is smaller than a sparrow, so it can easily dart in and out of leaves and branches. With its strong muscles and bladelike wings it can move up or down, sideways or backward, or hover in front of a flower. Then, with its long thin beak it drinks the nectar deep inside the blossoms.

Amazing! thought Howard. A special bird made just for this place.

While Howard was spying on the hummingbird, he got the feeling that something was spying on him. And when he looked he saw that he had company — a little black spider monkey was watching him with big, curious eyes.

Spider monkeys live together in bands, moving through the jungle by swinging rapidly from branch to branch with their long tails and hands. Sometimes they spread their arms and legs and just drop from one tree to another. They stay up in the trees where they have everything they need, and rarely touch the ground.

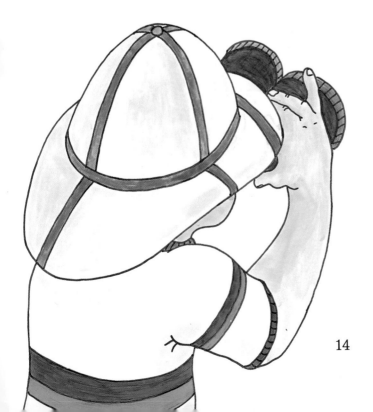

Some people think monkeys make good pets, but
Howard knew it was best to leave the wide-eyed little
fellow where he belonged, and continue his journey.

Back in the balloon, Howard pulled on the red handle that sent the fire roaring and the balloon soaring once more. Soon he left the green jungle far behind and flew out over the open grasslands.

The savannah is home to animals like elephants and lions, buffalo and antelope — animals that love to roam far and wide. Some, like the zebras he could see below him, travel in really large herds — a thousand or more!

It's a good thing they have so much space, thought Howard. This way each animal has all the room it needs. But then, that was surely the way God had planned it — each animal had its own special place.

Zebras need a good long drink every day. Their stripes help them blend into the shadows as they stand drinking — which is good, if you're a zebra and have to worry about lions sneaking up on you.

It is often dry and dusty on the savannah, and seeing the zebras with their noses in the cool water made Howard thirsty.

Howard poked into the travel chest for something to drink. He was happy to find a flask of water and right next to it a knapsack full of sandwiches and apples.

So Howard had a drink and a snack while he watched the zebras at the water-hole. Then he climbed back into the basket and settled down to see where the balloon would take him next.

The wind carried him so swiftly that, when he looked down again, the savannah was gone. All he saw was brown-gold sand stretching away below him in every direction.

In the daytime it can be very hot in the desert and, as the balloon came slowly down, Howard began feeling much too warm. So he took off his shirt and rolled up his jeans.

I wonder what kind of creatures can live in a place like this? he thought, as he slid over the side of the basket. He tied the balloon to a big rock, and hurried off to see what he could find.

Very little rain falls in the desert, making it extremely dry. Howard began to think that he wouldn't find any creatures here at all.

All the same, he had not taken more than a dozen steps when he met a lizard skittering across the sand. Many kinds of snakes and lizards make their home in the desert. They have adapted to the hot, dry climate and need very little water to drink. The lizard's tough, spiny skin is just the thing to keep water in and sand out.

"Well, you may be suited for the desert, but I'm not," said Howard. "It's back to the balloon for me!" Taking his place in the basket, Howard pulled on the red handle. The fire went WHOOSH! and the balloon floated away.

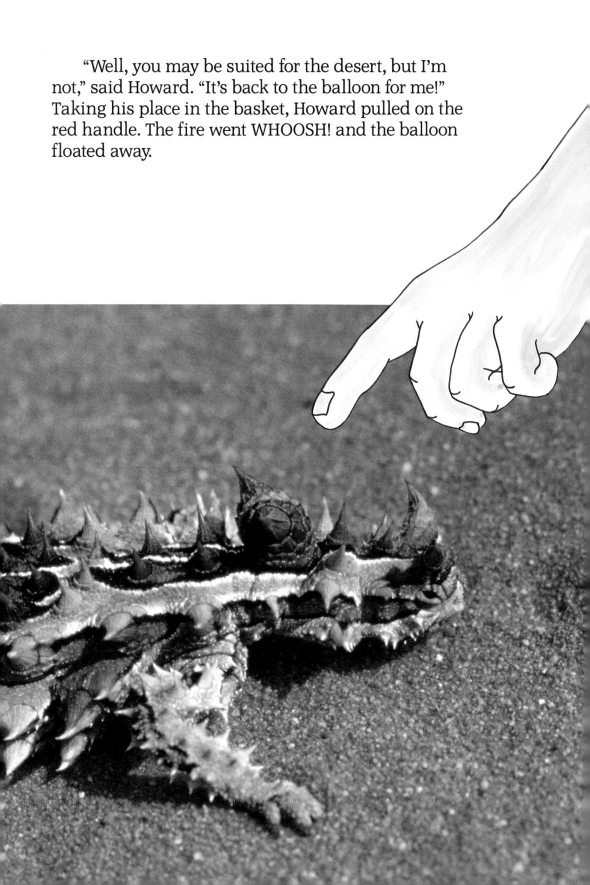

This time the balloon flew very high indeed.
Howard saw nothing but clouds, clouds and more
clouds. There must be something down there, he
thought, and decided to go for a closer look.

Down, down he went. At last the clouds cleared
away and he saw a bright, shining wilderness of white:
the brilliant white of thousands of miles of ice and snow.

Wow! I'm the first boy to reach the South Pole in a balloon, thought Howard, suddenly very cold. Quickly, he dug to the bottom of the chest where he found a heavy winter parka, warm boots and furry mittens.

Surely, nothing can live in such a cold place, he thought.

But Howard had no sooner climbed out of the basket than he saw a group of dignified little gentlemen in dinner jackets hurrying toward him over the ice and snow.

"Of course!" cried Howard. "Penguins!"

With their thick, downy coats — well padded with blubber — penguins can live in cold that would freeze other animals. They did not seem at all afraid, so Howard thought of a follow-the-leader game they could play, and away they went, hopping and waddling across the ice.

Howard could have stayed and played with the
penguins for hours, but he saw the sun sinking lower
and knew that it was time to go. So, waving goodbye to
the penguins, he climbed back into the basket and soon
he was floating out over the great blue ocean once more.

The sun was setting when Howard came within sight of his home again.

"What a day I've had," he said to himself, thinking of all the places he had seen — each as different as different could be.

Yet he had seen how each animal he had met was specially created for each place. A lizard could never live at the icy South Pole, and a penguin could not live in a desert, but each is happy in its own home.

In fact, God has created a place for every living thing on earth, and each one is made for its own special place.

I had to put on a parka to keep warm, and take off my shirt to keep cool, thought Howard. But by changing what I wear, I can fit in anywhere, too.

And that was also the way God made it.

Text and illustrations copyright © 1988 Steve Lawhead

Published by
Lion Publishing Corporation
1705 Hubbard Avenue, Batavia, Illinois 60510, USA
ISBN 0 7459 1268 0
Lion Publishing plc
Icknield Way, Tring, Herts, England
ISBN 0 7459 1268 0
Albatross Books Pty Ltd
PO Box 320, Sutherland, NSW 2232, Australia
ISBN 0 86760 923 0

First edition 1988

Acknowledgments
The photographs in this book have been supplied by
Bruce Coleman Limited, except the following:
Ace Photo Agency pp. 4-5, 20-21, 28-29
Barnaby's Picture Library pp. 6-7, 24-25, 26-27
ZEFA (UK) Ltd pp. 22-23

Library of Congress Cataloging-in-Publication Data
Lawhead, Steve
   Howard had a hot air balloon
   "A Lion book."
   [1. Hot air balloons — Fiction. 2 Balloon ascensions —
Fiction. 3. Christian life — Fiction] I. Title.
   PZ7.L41847H1 1988   [E]   87-17022
   ISBN 0-7459-1268-0

British Library Cataloguing-in-Publication Data
Lawhead, Steve
   Howard had a hot air balloon
   I. Title
   813'.54 [J]   PZ7
   ISBN 0 7459 1268 0

Printed in Hong Kong